The
Loneliest
Kitten

The Loneliest Kitten

by Holly Webb

Illustrated by Sophy Williams

tiger tales

tiger tales

5 River Road, Suite 128, Wilton, CT 06897
Published in the United States 2020
Originally published in Great Britain 2019
by the Little Tiger Group
Text copyright © 2019 Holly Webb
Illustrations copyright © 2019 Sophy Williams
Author photograph © Charlotte Knee Photography
ISBN-13: 978-1-68010-456-1
ISBN-10: 1-68010-456-X
Printed in China
STP/1800/0309/1119
10 9 8 7 6 5 4 3 2

For more insight and activities, visit us at www.tigertalesbooks.com

Contents

For everyone at Birch Copse Primary School

Chapter One
The Surprise

"Take off your sneakers!" Mom yelped as Darcy and Will reached the back door.

"Sorry, Mom." Darcy kicked off her sneakers and held on to Will's arm so he could do the same. Even though it was the beginning of summer vacation, the weather wasn't very summery. "The yard is really wet, and it's all muddy in front of the soccer goal...."

"I can see that. Will looks like he's been rolling in it."

"I was the goalkeeper!" Will said enthusiastically.

Dad came into the kitchen and stared at Darcy and Will. "Wow. What happened to you two?"

"We were playing soccer." Darcy frowned. "You're home early."

"That's why I called you in," said

Mom. *She has an "I've got a secret" face on*, Darcy thought. "You'd better go and get changed. And Will, I think you probably need a shower. We're going on a trip, somewhere really exciting, but it's a surprise."

"I'm here so I can come, too," Dad added. "I wish I'd been here earlier. Then I could have joined in your soccer game. I'm almost as good a goalie as Will!"

"Nobody is better than me," Will said smugly. "I saved almost all of Darcy's shots."

Darcy made a face over the top of Will's head to say that he hadn't really, and Mom smiled. Will was actually very good for someone who was only six. He was tall, too—not that much shorter than Darcy, and she was three years older.

"Go and get changed, Darcy," said Mom. "And don't worry, there's no need to dress up. Shorts and a T-shirt are fine."

"Come on, Will, I'll turn the shower on for you," Dad suggested.

Darcy could hear Will trying to quiz Dad as they went upstairs. "Where are we going? Will there be pizza? Can I wear my Batman outfit?" She was curious, too. They did sometimes go on surprise day trips during the summer— the best one had been to the ocean, with huge pieces of pizza on the boardwalk— but that was usually for the whole day, not in the middle of the afternoon.

She hurried into her bedroom and

changed out of her muddy sweatpants and soccer shirt. Luckily Mom had put her hair in braids that morning and it still looked okay, even after playing soccer. She just had to scrub away the mud from under her fingernails.

Will was back downstairs soon after, looking very clean and a little damp.

"Where are we going?" he kept asking as Mom and Dad hurried them out to the car.

"*Shh*," Darcy whispered. "It's a surprise. Surprises are good. Don't spoil it."

"I want to *know*," her little brother muttered crossly. "I don't like surprises."

"Five minutes," Dad promised from the driver's seat.

Darcy and Will peered eagerly out

the car windows, trying to figure out where they might be going—Darcy thought they were close to where her friend Emma lived. Then a few minutes later, Dad pulled up outside a long, low building.

Darcy read the sign outside: Haven Animal Rescue. She unclipped her seat belt and reached over to grab Dad's shoulder. "Are we ... do you mean ... are we really—" She swallowed hard and started again. "Are we going to get a cat?"

"A cat!" Will squeaked.

Darcy had been trying to persuade her parents to get a pet for such a long time. She hadn't been sure whether they should get a cat or a dog.

Emma had a dog, and she kept

telling Darcy about all the naughty things he had done. Buster had eaten two of Emma's lunch boxes (not what was inside them, the actual box!) and her favorite flip-flops. Emma still loved him a lot, but he was a handful.

Darcy and Will's grandma loved cats, and she had two beautiful ones. When they went to see Grandma, if Darcy was very lucky, Pansy or Smudge might get on her knee. Darcy loved it when they sat there and let her pet them. It would be amazing to have a cat to play with all the time. A cat of their own might even decide to sleep on Darcy's bed.

Mom loved cats, too, but Dad wasn't convinced—he said they would need a lot of care.

"I thought you'd said no!" Darcy

wrapped her arms around Dad's neck and hugged him.

"Well, I realized it's Mom who's at home most of the time," Dad pointed out. "She'll end up taking care of it, so she should be the one to make the decision."

Dad is right, Darcy thought. Her mom worked from home in a little office.

"But we'll help," she said eagerly. "We can feed the cat. And I can vacuum up the fur." Cat hair all over the carpets had been one of the things Dad was concerned about. "I like vacuuming," she assured him.

"Can we go and see the cat *now*?" Will begged, and Dad laughed and opened the car door.

"Come on!"

"We made an appointment to see a litter of kittens," Mom explained as they went into the building. "There are four of them, and they're old enough to be adopted now. When you went over to Grandma's the other day, a lady from the rescue came to check the house to make sure we weren't too close to any busy streets or anything like that. They called me yesterday to say we can definitely have a kitten! But—" she gave Darcy and Will a serious look—"they only allow pets to be adopted by people who have older children, because you need to be sensible to be around a cat or a dog. So you must show them how sensible you can be. No arguing!"

Will's eyes widened, and he nodded seriously.

"Hi, I'm Lucy Adams." Mom smiled at the woman behind the reception desk. "We're here to see some kittens."

"Yes! We're expecting you. Wait here for a minute, and Jesse will come and get you—he's one of our staff. We have a meeting room where you can get to know the kittens before you choose."

Choose! Darcy looked around the

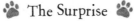

reception area at the photos of cats and dogs on the walls. They were beautiful, and all of them were staring hopefully out of the picture, as if begging to be taken home.

How were they going to choose which kitten should be theirs?

A young man in a green fleece with the Haven logo came in and grinned at Darcy and Will. "Hi—you're here to meet the kittens?"

"That's right." Mom squeezed Darcy's hand. "We're really excited."

"Great. They're in our meeting room down here." Jesse led them along a hallway lined with more adorable photos and opened a door. "It's okay, they're shut in," he explained as Dad peered in, looking a little worried.

"They aren't going to make a run for it."

"Oh, look…," Mom said softly as she went in. "Aren't they sweet, Darcy?"

But Darcy didn't say anything. She was too busy watching. Jesse was unlatching a wire crate, and three tiny kittens were starting to nose curiously at the door. They climbed and wriggled and stomped all over each other, trying to get out and see what was going on.

"Look at the orange one!" Will gasped as an orange and white striped kitten launched itself over the top of two tabbies, bouncing onto the floor. It sniffed nosily at Dad's sneakers and then batted one paw at the dangling laces.

The tabby kittens stumbled out behind the orange one and gazed thoughtfully up at Mom and Darcy.

"Do they know we want to take one of them home?" Darcy whispered to her mom.

"You're actually the first family these kittens have met," Jesse said, "so they probably don't know what's going on. We've had them for a few weeks, with their mom. We're planning to get her adopted with one of the kittens, and the others either on their own or together."

"Just one for us!" Dad said anxiously. "We're not very experienced pet owners. We only want one kitten."

Darcy closed her mouth firmly. She'd been just about to say that maybe they should have two kittens, but she didn't want Dad to reconsider getting a cat.

"Aren't there four of them?" she asked Jesse, looking around the room. There were definitely only three kittens out. The two tabbies were still by the crate, watching cautiously, and the orange one was now trying to climb up Dad's jeans.

Jesse nodded. "Look...," he said, and Darcy crouched down to look inside the wire crate. It was padded with a

rumpled fleece
blanket, and
peering out
from under
the folds was
a small, worried-
looking tabby and white face.

Chapter Two
Meeting the Kittens

The kitten had the pinkest nose that Darcy had ever seen on a cat. It was such a bright pink that it almost looked like it would glow in the dark. The kitten stared back at Darcy with round, yellow-green eyes, and then it stepped out from under the folds of the blanket. Now Darcy could see that it looked different from the other two tabbies. They were tabby all over, with gray-brown paws. This kitten was tabby with a neat white shirt front and sparklingly white paws. It had a very cute white chin, too, as if it was white with a tabby mask over its eyes and ears.

"Oh, that's a very sweet kitten," Mom said, and Jesse laughed.

"I know—I love his markings."

The tabby and white kitten edged slowly out of the crate and then sat down in front of it. He still looked nervous—*maybe he's scared of the room full of people*, Darcy thought. Will was so desperate to make Jesse think he was sensible that he hadn't said a word, but even though they were being quiet, they were still very big compared to a kitten.

The kitten lifted one of his front paws, licked at it, and passed it vaguely in the direction of his ears. Darcy had a feeling he wasn't really trying to wash; it was just giving him something to do, so he could pretend he hadn't noticed all these people staring at him.

Now that he was washing, Darcy noticed the underside of his paws—the pads were the same neon-pink as his nose. They stood out brightly against the white fur, like little pink beans.

"He's so handsome," she said, looking hopefully at Mom to see if she felt the same way. Maybe she'd fallen in love with one of the others....

But Mom was looking at the kitten who was washing, too, with the same sort of face that Darcy imagined she was making. "Isn't he?" she agreed.

"He's washing his *ears*," Will said in a tiny whisper. "He's so smart!"

Dad sighed. "I take it we're adopting this one, then?"

"Don't you like him?" Darcy asked indignantly.

"Um.... He's definitely cute," Dad admitted. "I'm just not a big cat person."

"I'm sorry," Darcy said to Jesse, hoping this didn't put him off them.

"It's okay." Jesse grinned. "I'm pretty sure this one will win your dad over."

They walked back to the car with the kitten in a cat carrier. It had been in the trunk of the car the whole time, but Darcy and Will hadn't known. Mom told them she had been to the pet store and bought it the same day the rescue had done the home check. She'd bought a cat basket, some food bowls, and kitten food, too. They were all hidden in the shed in the yard.

"I didn't buy any toys or a collar yet, though. I thought you two would like to help choose those," she said.

"What will the kitten play with when we get home?" Will asked, frowning.

"Kittens play with everything." Mom laughed. "You saw that orange one trying to eat Dad's shoelaces. They like pieces of string, balls of paper. Sunbeams, even. Don't worry. I expect our kitten will be too busy exploring to miss having any toys."

Our kitten. Darcy smiled—it sounded so good. She watched as Mom settled the cat carrier on the back seat between her and Will. Darcy could just see the kitten through the spaces in the sides. He was huddled up in a little ball at the end, and he didn't look very happy.

"It's okay," Darcy whispered as Mom started the car. "I bet you don't like being shut up in there. But we'll be home soon, and then you can get out."

From inside the carrier, the kitten heard her whispering, but he didn't know what she meant. He didn't like this. The carrier had been swinging around, and now it was moving strangely, so that his insides felt like they were being left behind. The car skidded to a stop, and the carrier shook. The kitten slid forward with a little mew of fright.

28

The carrier had a soft blanket on the bottom, folded up like a cushion. He remembered a blanket like that from the crate back at the rescue. It was soft and warm, and inside it would be dark. He'd feel safe in there, he decided. He patted at the edge of the blanket with his claws, ruffling it up into a fold so he could sneak underneath. It made a cozy little cave, and he crept inside.

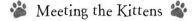

"I don't think he liked being in the car," Darcy said, looking worriedly at the small hump of blanket that was the kitten. "He mewed when we had to stop at the lights, and then he hid in the blanket." They had put the carrier

29

down in the corner of the kitchen, but the kitten didn't seem to want to come out.

"Poor little thing," Mom said, crouching down to look at the rumpled blanket. "I did try to drive as slowly as I could. But I suppose he's never been in a car before. He'll be okay soon. Right now, though, I think we need to be patient and just leave him alone."

Darcy nodded. She knew Mom was right, even though she was desperate to play with the kitten. Jesse had told them that the kittens had been born at the rescue after their mom had been found abandoned. They'd never been anywhere else. Their kitten must feel like everything was different and scary. No wonder he wanted to stay wrapped up in a blanket.

"Maybe he'll come out if we put out food for him," Will suggested hopefully.

"He's in a blanket!" Darcy pointed out. "He won't see the food."

"But he might be able to smell it," Mom said thoughtfully. "It's worth a try. We want him to like being here, so feeding him would be a good start."

She picked up the bag of kitten food and shook some of the pieces into the kitten's new bowl. It rattled as the food fell in, and Darcy saw the blanket twitch.

The kitten was thinking. He knew that noise, and he was hungry. But outside the warm, safe cocoon of blanket there were different smells and the oddness of being away from his mother and the other kittens. Did he want to come out?

He was *very* hungry, though. He could smell the food now—the scent was creeping across the kitchen, and it was making him feel even hungrier. His nose poked out from under the fold of blanket, and he eyed the open door of the carrier. He could see the bowl right there, with the girl and boy sitting on the floor behind it.

When they saw him watching, the girl patted the boy's arm and they edged backward, leaving a little more space between them and the bowl. That was better. It wasn't quite as scary if they weren't so close.

The kitten stumbled out over the folds of blanket and stood hesitantly in the doorway of the carrier. Then he crept over to the bowl and started to eat, keeping one eye on the children. It seemed like such a long time since he'd last been fed, and there was a good bowlful here. He had to go more slowly toward the end, and he even left a few pieces of food. He then sat down heavily and ran his paw over his whiskers.

He could see the children looking at him. They seemed a lot less scary now that they'd been sitting still for so long and he was feeling much better after the food, although now he was a little sleepy. Thoughtfully, he padded toward them and sniffed at the girl's hands. She was less scary than the boy since she kept so still. The boy wriggled. The girl didn't move, even when the kitten licked at her fingers—she shivered a little, that was all.

The kitten sat down. He was very full and he was feeling sleepy, and the girl's foot was in just the right place for his chin to lean on. He slumped against her and then, seconds later, he let out a tiny kitten snore.

Chapter Three
Settling in at Home

"Oh, Charlie! Where's your collar?"

"Not another one!" Mom turned around, and Darcy held up the kitten to show her. Charlie nuzzled happily against her fingers.

"Look—no collar."

"I don't know how he does it." Mom stared at Charlie and shook her head. "You silly," she said lovingly. "It's lucky

I bought you a spare last time, isn't it? Hold on to him a minute, Darcy, and I'll get the new one."

The kitten had settled in well after his shy start. He was funny and clever, and Mom was right that he would play with anything. He adored Dad, too. He seemed to know that Dad wasn't as much of a cat fan, so he had to be the perfect pet. Whenever Dad sat on the couch, Charlie would appear as if by magic. Then he'd try to climb up the side of his jeans so he could collapse exhausted on Dad's lap. Dad pretended it was nothing, but Darcy could tell he loved it. He'd pet Charlie over and over, running one finger all the way down from the top of his head to his tail.

They had argued for a long time over what to call him. Will thought he should be called Mario, like the video game character, but Darcy didn't think he looked like a Mario. He needed something that was cuddly but showed his mischievous side, too. Like the way he could get onto the kitchen table in less than ten seconds and drink the milk out of her cereal bowl before she was back from the fridge with a glass of juice.

It was actually Dad who came up with the name. He said the kitten reminded him of someone he'd gone to school with—his friend Charlie was always getting into trouble, but then he'd look really innocent and sorry, and everyone forgave him. Dad suggested it just after the kitten had thrown up on his shoe.

Charlie's worst trick was getting rid of his collar. "How did you do it this time?" Darcy asked, tickling him under the chin. "I'll look for it in the yard later, Mom."

Ever since Charlie had been old enough to go outside, Darcy and Will had been finding collars in the flower beds, and Hannah, who lived next door, had come over with one that had been in her lavender bush. Charlie seemed to have a gift for hooking his collar on things. The collars had special catches that came open if the cat was trapped or caught on something, and Charlie had figured out exactly how to get rid of them.

He wriggled as Mom clipped on another collar, and Darcy was sure he glared at her. He was probably figuring out how to get himself out of this one.

"Do you have your bag packed and ready for tomorrow, Darcy?"

"No." Darcy sighed. She was looking forward to going back to school and seeing everyone, but after seven weeks of vacation, it was going to be hard getting up early every morning. And it was going to be even harder leaving Charlie behind after spending all those weeks playing with him. "Charlie's going to miss us, Mom.

You must promise you'll give him lots of attention, even when you're working."

Mom laughed. "Yes, of course I will. I don't think I'll have a choice anyway. He'll be up on my desk stomping around on my keyboard, I bet."

"I suppose...," Darcy agreed. "I'll go and sort out my stuff now, and I'll take Charlie with me."

Darcy carried the kitten up to her room and put him on her bed. She watched, smiling, as Charlie stomped up and down the comforter, his paws sinking in with every step. Then he peered thoughtfully over the edge of her bed and scrambled down the side to explore the bedroom.

Darcy got her school backpack out
of the closet. Mom had bought her
new pencils and notebooks a couple
of weeks before, but she had forgotten
where she'd put them—her room was
a bit of a mess. Charlie stalked a ball
of paper across the carpet and went
wriggling under the bed for a while.
He came out with his white parts all
covered in fluffy dust, and Darcy had
to brush him off.

"You're so funny," she whispered as she blew dust off his whiskers and he sneezed and almost fell over. "I'm going to miss you, but I promise I'll come home right after school. We'll spend time playing with you then. And Emma's going to come over, too. You like her, don't you?"

Charlie climbed onto Darcy's lap and curled up there, batting sleepily at the ends of her hair. Darcy sighed. Even though Mom had promised to try, Charlie was going to be so bored without her and Will to play with.

"Mom! Mom! Guess what!" Darcy came flying out of school that first afternoon with Emma dashing behind her. She flung herself gleefully at her mom.

"I can't imagine," Mom said, staggering backward. "What happened?"

"Mrs. Jennings is organizing a girls' soccer team—and me and Emma are going to be on it! It's in a school league and everything! There'll be practice on Tuesdays and Thursdays, and games, too. That's okay, isn't it? I can do it, can't I? There's a form you have to sign. Mrs. Jennings even showed us the uniform—it's green—it's so cool, Mom!"

"Wow! Yes…. That should be fine, I think. Luckily it doesn't overlap with swimming on Wednesdays. You're going to be busy!"

"I can do it, though, can't I, Mom?" Emma asked her mom hopefully, and she nodded.

"Of course. Great job, you two!"

"It's going to be amazing!" Darcy hugged Emma, and they danced around until Will came across the playground, looking a little tired and grumpy.

"We're going to be on the soccer team!" Darcy told him excitedly.

"Oh—great. Can we go home and see Charlie now?"

Darcy blinked. Just for those few minutes since Mrs. Jennings had come to their classroom at the end of school, she'd completely forgotten about Charlie—on the very first day they'd left him alone. She suddenly felt guilty.

"Was he okay today, Mom?" she asked anxiously.

"I think so. He played with the cat dancer toy, and then he slept on my knee while I was working. Still, he'll be happy to see you two."

Darcy nodded. "We'll play with him for a long time when we get home."

"Don't forget your soccer practice," Emma reminded her. "Mrs. Jennings said we need to practice at home, too."

45

Charlie hopped down the stairs a step at a time as he heard them coming up the path. He'd spent most of the day asleep, occasionally wandering around the house looking for Darcy and Will. Their mom was in her little office near the stairs, but she just kept typing around him, even when he tried to catch her fingers to nibble. It wasn't much fun.

As the front door opened, he galloped across the hallway and twined lovingly in and out of Darcy's and Will's legs. They crouched down and petted him, and Darcy rubbed his ears just the way he liked it. Charlie purred and purred— he'd missed them so much.

He followed the children eagerly as

they went into the kitchen and accepted
a little bit of Darcy's cheese sandwich.
Where had they been all day? They'd
never gone away for so long before.
Charlie bounced around excitedly as
Darcy waved the cat dancer
toy. It was his
favorite—he
loved stalking it
up the hallway,
but every time
he pounced,
Darcy would
whisk it up
out of the
way, so
that his
paws just
grazed the dancing feathers. He had

more of a chance when he played with Will, as sometimes Will wasn't quick enough and Charlie managed to get a mouthful of feathers.

But after they'd played for a little while, Darcy disappeared upstairs and came down in different clothes. She was going into the yard, Charlie realized, and he hurried out the door after her. He loved being outside. There were so many good hiding places and interesting smells in the yard. Sometimes there were bees, too, and butterflies. Charlie was desperate to catch a fat furry bumblebee. They blundered around just in front of his nose, but somehow, he'd never managed to nab one.

Whatever Darcy was doing was probably even more interesting than

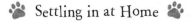

a bee, though. He followed her across the lawn and sprang delightedly on the soccer ball when she tapped it with her foot and it rolled across the grass. She laughed and tapped it again and he raced after the ball, flinging himself on top of it and then rolling off onto the grass. He sprang up and lunged again as Darcy sent the ball across the grass, and this time as the ball rolled, he went with it, nosediving to the ground.

Darcy crouched down next to him. She looked at him worriedly as he shook his whiskers. "I'm sorry, Charlie. Did it squish you? Are you okay? Maybe I'd better take you inside, kitten. I don't want you to get hurt."

She scooped him up and slipped him back inside the kitchen door, and then she flipped the switch on the cat flap so he couldn't follow her back out again.

Charlie glared indignantly at the cat flap. Darcy had been away all day, and now he wasn't allowed out to play with her! He stalked across the kitchen and sat down grumpily in his basket. Why had Darcy stopped him from playing? He'd only wanted to be with her. What had he done wrong?

Chapter Four
A New Friend

Charlie could see the children were going to disappear the next day, too— they had bags and coats and everything was a rush. When he tried to get on the table to drink the milk out of Will's cereal bowl, Mom scooped him back down with a firm, "No!" and then she added, "Oh, no, he's lost his collar again! I'll have to get him another one."

Darcy made a fuss of him when she gave him his breakfast, but she was dashing around and didn't want to play. Charlie went to sit a little way up the stairs and watched as the children pulled on their shoes. Why were they leaving again?

When Will ran back into the kitchen to grab his forgotten lunch box, Charlie padded softly down the stairs and sniffed at his backpack, trying to figure out what was happening. The zipper was open, and the bag smelled strange—musty, like leftover packed lunches. It was interesting…. Charlie put one paw in, and then the other, and sniffed at the grubby crumbs at the bottom of the bag. Then he sneezed.

"Look at Charlie! He's in my bag!"

Charlie looked up to see Will crouching over him, laughing.

"I think he wants to come to school!"

"Poor Charlie—he's missing you," Mom said. "You'd better get him out, Will. We need to go."

Charlie wriggled as Will gently

reached under his front legs and lifted him out of the bag. Taking him out only made him think that the bag was exciting....

He watched gloomily as the front door slammed behind them, and then stalked back into the kitchen to his basket.

Maybe they'd play with him when they got home....

Darcy and Will did their best to fit in taking care of Charlie with all their school stuff. But Darcy was really excited about being on the soccer team. She'd always loved kicking a ball around, but now she was seriously trying to practice her soccer skills. And it wasn't just practicing—she gotten Dad to take her to the library to find books about soccer, too. If she wasn't outside playing soccer, she was curled up on the couch reading about it.

A couple of weeks after the quarter had started, Charlie padded into the living room to see if Darcy would play with him. She and Will had just gotten back from school, and he was so happy to see them. He snuggled up between Darcy and the cushions for a while, but he'd been dozing for most of the day, and he wanted to run around and chase things, not help her read. He tried patting at the pages and even sitting on the book, but she just kept moving him. In the end he jumped down from the couch and went to see what Will was doing.

Charlie could hear him growling as he came into the kitchen. Will was glaring at a worksheet on the table—then he started to erase what he'd just written and ended up throwing the eraser halfway across the table so it bounced onto the floor.

A game! At last!

Charlie sprang at it, batting the eraser with his paw and enjoying the way his claws caught in it.

"Hey! I need that!" Will reached down and grabbed it back. "I'm sorry, Charlie. I hate homework. It's the worst thing about first grade." He looked at Charlie again. "You've lost *another* collar! I'd better tell Mom."

Charlie sat under Will's chair, hoping that he might throw the eraser again, but he didn't. In the end, the little kitten gave up on him and popped through the cat flap out into the yard. Maybe today would be the day he caught a bumblebee.

He padded across the grass, twitching happily as he felt the hot sun on his fur. He sat down in the middle of the lawn and washed his ears for a bit—and then all of a sudden, *there* was a bee!

57

It zoomed wildly across the grass in front of him, swooping down to a patch of clover. Charlie went into a hunting crouch and tried to stalk it, but the bee lumbered away before he even got close. He hurried after it, chasing it over to the lavender bush by the wall until it disappeared into the yard next door, buzzing happily.

Charlie stared after it, his tail twitching. He could still hear the buzzing. He'd been so close! Suddenly determined, he jumped up onto the bench and then made a wobbly leap onto the wooden back. He teetered there for a moment and then sprang for the wall, scratching hard and digging his claws into the branches of ivy. Then he was on the top of the wall, with the bee buzzing lazily across the flower beds below him.

Charlie made a rushing, scrambling climb down the other side of the wall and looked around for the bee. The fur on his back was rumpled up with the wild scramble down the wall and a little bit with fright. He hadn't expected it to be quite so high. But now, surely, he'd catch that bee!

Except it had disappeared. It was completely, utterly gone. Charlie looked around in disbelief. It wasn't fair!

A soft murmuring noise made his ears twitch—but it wasn't a bee. It was someone talking. Whoever it was had a pleasant, gentle sort of voice, a bit like Darcy when she was petting him.

Curiously, Charlie padded down to the fence at the end of the yard next door and saw that there were gaps along the bottom of it—quite big gaps. He could get through there easily, no scrambling needed. He wriggled through and hesitated in the bushes, watching an elderly lady watering her flowers. She was muttering to herself about the weather, which was warm and dry now after the wet summer.

The water drops glinted and sparkled in the sunshine, and he padded a little closer. The lady didn't see him; she just kept watering, and Charlie couldn't resist the pattering of the drops any longer. He pounced, springing at the glittering water, trying to catch the drops with his white paws.

"Oh! Where did you come from?" the lady gasped. "Oh, dear, are you all wet now?"

Charlie had water droplets covering his whiskers, up his nose, and in his ears. He shook his head briskly and then looked hopefully up at her. Was she going to do it again? He reached one paw up and tapped at the watering can.

"You liked it?" Laughing, the lady

tipped up the watering can and let another shower of droplets fall down on the plants—and the kitten. Charlie batted his paws eagerly, but still he couldn't catch the water.

"I wonder where you came from," the lady said thoughtfully. "I haven't seen you before. I'd remember that beautiful tabby pattern." She reached down and gently rubbed the top of the kitten's head. "You don't look like you're lost. You're definitely someone's pet; you're so friendly. But you don't have a collar on…."

Charlie tapped the watering can again and she sprinkled a little more water on her patio, laughing as he danced around and tried to catch the water. At last she set it down by an outside tap and walked slowly back inside. Charlie padded after her. He liked this lady. She was fussing over him just the way he wanted, and the water was a lot of fun.

"Oh, no, I don't think you should come inside, little one," she said gently. "You're someone else's kitten, and they wouldn't want you coming in, would they? You go on back home now."

She closed the glass door and stood just inside it, watching him. Charlie stared back and then stood up, putting his front paws on the glass and peering through. He mewed sadly and saw the lady put her hand on the couch and try to crouch down to look at him. Then she shook her head firmly, stood up, and walked away.

Charlie sat down on the patio and

wailed. He wanted her to come out and play again. *No one* would play with him. He was so lonely....

Five minutes later, Charlie was inside the lady's living room, sitting on the arm of the couch and nibbling a little cube of cheese.

Chapter Five
A Busy Day

"Yes!" Darcy ran back to high-five Bella, who'd set up her goal. "Three-one!" She waved jubilantly at Mom and Emma, who were standing at the edge of the pitch. Emma was jumping up and down. Mrs. Jennings was trying to make sure everyone had a turn playing, especially since this was their first real game, but Darcy felt bad that Emma hadn't gotten to play for longer. She didn't seem to be upset about it, though.

Darcy had been really worried when Mrs. Jennings told them about the game—after all, they'd only been a team for three weeks, and they definitely needed more practice. But Mrs. Jennings promised it would be really good experience, even if they lost. And now they were winning! All that skills training Darcy had been doing in the park after school had made a difference. When the final whistle blew, the score was four-two, and the Willow Elementary team just couldn't stop talking about the game.

"Should we go to the store and get a celebration cake?" Mom suggested as Darcy got into the car. "I saw some the other day that had soccer balls on them."

"Yes, please!" Darcy leaned back in the front seat, exhausted but beaming. She loved the idea of a special celebration. "I can't wait for Sunday," she added happily. Mrs. Jennings had arranged another game with a local school for that Sunday afternoon.

"Can we get Charlie some cat treats, too?" she asked as they took the cake to the checkout. "I think we're out of them."

"Sure—I think they're in that aisle." Mom pointed, and Darcy hurried off.

"They were on sale, three for two, so I got all the flavors," she explained as she came back and put them in the basket.

When they got home, Darcy went to take a shower and then came down for a piece of cake. She opened the bag of cheese-flavored cat treats and shook them. That always made Charlie come running—he knew exactly what the noise meant!

Nothing happened and Darcy shook the bag again, this time next to the open kitchen window. She expected to see a little tabby and white blur come dashing across the yard to bang the cat flap open, but still nothing. She stood in the middle of the kitchen with the bag, looking lost.

"Mom, where's Charlie?"

Her mom looked up from cutting the soccer cake and glanced around the kitchen. "I bet he's in the yard. I should put his food down, actually. I forgot we haven't fed him yet."

"So ... he hasn't eaten?" Darcy said, frowning. No dinner, and he wasn't coming for his favorite cat treats? That was definitely strange, and worrying....

Darcy looked all around the house for Charlie—she wondered if Mom had accidentally shut him in one of the bedrooms. But she couldn't see him anywhere. She stood in the yard and called for him, but no kitten appeared.

Mom went to look up and down the street at the front of the house. Charlie had wandered down the side path of the house before, and Darcy had found him sunbathing on the front wall. Will searched upstairs again, even going through all his toy baskets.

"I wonder where he could have

gone," Mom said as she came back in. "He's usually good at showing up for meals, although...."

"What?" Darcy asked anxiously. "Although what, Mom?"

"Have you noticed that Charlie hasn't been around as much over the past week? And he hasn't been climbing on me while I'm working."

Darcy shook her head. "No. He's always here when we get home from school." Then she was silent for a minute. *Was* he? Would she definitely have noticed? She'd been so busy with after-school soccer and all the extra practice she was doing. "Mom, do you think something's happened to him?"

"I'm sure he's fine," her mom said

encouragingly, but there was still no Charlie.

Darcy was just starting to get really panicky when the kitten appeared, popping in through the cat flap and strolling calmly across the kitchen. He looked surprised when Darcy swooped down and picked him up for a hug.

"We didn't know where you were!" she told him, rubbing his ears.

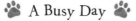

Charlie blinked at her and nudged her chin with his chilly little nose. "Are you hungry?" Darcy asked him. She kept him cuddled in one arm and used the other hand to get the bag of kitten food out of the cupboard.

Mom took over and poured food into Charlie's bowl. Darcy had expected him to leap down at once and start eating, but he didn't seem very interested. He just sniffed at the bag as she got it out, that was all. When she put him down next to the bowl, he only nibbled a couple of mouthfuls, and then he sat next to the food and started to wash himself. He didn't seem to be hungry at all.

"Maybe he doesn't like it," Will suggested, looking down at the cat food. "I wouldn't. It smells horrible."

"He's liked it until now," Darcy said. "Why would he suddenly change his mind?"

"Actually, I've noticed he hasn't been eating the whole bowl recently," Mom said. "Maybe we should cut down on how much we're giving him. If he's not growing quite as fast now that he's a little older, maybe he's not as hungry."

"Maybe...." Darcy sighed. She couldn't help feeling that there was more to it. But at least it was Friday, and she could keep a really careful eye on Charlie over the weekend. They didn't have much planned until her soccer game on Sunday afternoon, so she could spend a lot of time with him.

"Darcy, what *are* you doing?" Mom called out the kitchen window.

"I'm trying to teach Charlie how to be a stunt cat," Darcy yelled back. "He high-fived me! Did you see?"

"I can see him eating a lot of cat treats," Mom said a minute or so later.

"That's how the training works. You reward them every time they get it right. Or almost right. He's very clever," Darcy said lovingly, holding out her hand for Charlie to tap. He sniffed at her hopefully, looking for another treat.

"Okay…. Just don't feed him the whole bag!"

The website she'd been reading had said only to do five-minute training sessions, Darcy remembered. She didn't want Charlie to get annoyed. "You're a very good boy," she told him, putting the treats in her pocket. "What should we do now, hmm?"

She'd been trying to keep an eye on him all day, but she was beginning to think that they'd been worrying for nothing. Charlie had eaten almost all of his breakfast, and then she'd played with him, rolling a jingly ball up and down the hallway. He'd snoozed on the arm of the couch for a while. Then he'd stalked a feather around her bedroom floor while she'd done her homework. Will had taken him downstairs and played with the cat dancer, and then Charlie had sat under the kitchen table during lunch looking hopeful. He *might* have gotten the end of a cheese sandwich.

Everything was fine.

Darcy turned as she heard footsteps behind her and saw Will coming out onto the patio.

"Play soccer with me?" Will asked coaxingly. "Please, Darcy? I'm bored."

"Not right now. I'm trying to play with Charlie."

"You aren't. You're just sitting there."

"Is that my soccer ball you've got?" Darcy asked suspiciously. "That's my new one!"

"It was behind that flowerpot." Will shrugged. "You should put it away if it's so special."

"You're not playing with it," Darcy said firmly. "I'm serious."

"Don't be so mean!"

"Will, that's my new ball! Go and get your own!"

Will didn't answer. He smirked at Darcy and started to kick the ball against the wall.

"Mom!" Darcy yelled. "Make him stop playing with it!"

Will looked around to see if Mom was in the kitchen, listening, and lost control of the ball. It went flying over the back fence.

"Oh, now look what you've done!" Darcy said furiously. "We'll never get it back!"

"I'm sorry...," Will said guiltily. "I'll go over and ask for it."

"It's no good," Darcy snapped. "It didn't go next door into Hannah's yard. It went behind—that's the yard for the apartments. And we don't even know which apartment it belongs to." Then she stopped scowling at Will and turned slowly. "Where's Charlie?"

Will looked around the yard. "I don't know."

"But I was trying to watch him. I don't believe it—this is all your fault, Will!"

Charlie wriggled underneath the fence into the elderly lady's yard. He adored Darcy, especially when she was playing with him or he was snuggled up next to her in a fold of comforter at nighttime— but loud voices and shouting made him nervous and twitchy. He didn't like it when Darcy and Will argued. Every time they had an argument, the fur would start to prickle up along his spine, and his tail lashed. The elderly lady's basement apartment was always peaceful—there was no shouting. And she had cat treats now, too.

He padded across the yard and nosed hopefully at the glass door. It was shut, but one of the windows next to it was open a crack. He could definitely fit through there. He sprang up onto the

windowsill
and wriggled
his way in,
stepping
carefully
around
the photo
frames and
the vase on the inside. There
didn't seem to be anyone home, but
there was a patch of warm sunlight on
the rug, so he sat down in it and started
to lick his paws. He'd stay a while and
then maybe he'd go back and see if
Darcy wanted to play again. In a bit....

Chapter Six
Missing!

"He's been gone for so long," Darcy said miserably. "Hours, Mom. He never stays away this long. It's dinnertime, and usually he's starving. He's always sitting around looking hopeful long before we feed him."

Mom frowned. "Not for the last week or so, Darcy. Like I told you, he just doesn't seem as interested in his food anymore. That's why I cut down on how much I gave him for breakfast this morning."

Darcy stared at her. She vaguely remembered Mom saying something about that the day before when Charlie hadn't showed up in time for dinner, but she'd been more worried about where Charlie actually was, and she hadn't really been listening. Clearly she should have been.

"And you said he hadn't been around as much," she said. "He wasn't bothering you while you were working…. That's why I was trying to keep an eye on him today."

Her mom nodded. "I've missed him," she admitted with a worried smile. "I used to complain when he walked across the keyboard—he wasn't that helpful when I was trying to get people's accounts to balance, but actually he did make it a lot more fun...."

"And then he stopped doing it?"

"Yes.... I assumed it was because he was getting a little older and less playful. I just thought he was sleeping more." Mom nibbled her bottom lip and glanced at the cat flap as though she hoped Charlie might just pop through it.

He didn't.

"That makes sense, though," Dad said helpfully. "Cats sleep more when they're older, don't they?"

Darcy sat down on one of the kitchen chairs, her heart thumping fast. Charlie kept disappearing, and he wasn't as interested in his food. It was almost as if…. She looked down at her fingers, twisting them over and over. It was almost as if he didn't think their house was home anymore. He was going somewhere else. "Do you think he has another home?" she blurted out.

"What?" Will shook his head. "He couldn't." He sounded almost angry. "Don't say that, Darcy."

"Someone else who's feeding him and playing with him...," Darcy went on unhappily. She felt really guilty. She'd been so excited about getting their own kitten, and she and Will had made such a fuss over him those first weeks. They'd loved Charlie and played with him all the time. They'd carried him around, and they'd built him adventure playgrounds out of pillows and comfy beds whenever he'd looked the tiniest bit sleepy. They'd followed him anxiously once he was allowed out and started to explore the yard.

Then school had started again, and Darcy had been chosen for the soccer team—and suddenly there were more exciting things than kittens to think about.

But she'd *had* to practice, a little voice protested inside her. It was important! Well, it was—but she didn't need to have practiced *that* much, Darcy admitted to herself. And all those soccer books she'd borrowed from the library, because she had to be the best on the team....

Darcy winced as she remembered putting Charlie down on the floor because he would keep sitting on the exact diagram that she was trying to look at. He'd only wanted to play with her, she realized now. He hadn't understood—there had been so many weeks during summer vacation when she'd wanted to do nothing *but* play. And he'd thought they would keep going as before, and she'd been annoyed with him. She'd told him to stop it. Darcy felt tears pressing up behind her eyes, and she sniffed.

What about Will, though? There had been Will for Charlie to play with, the little voice inside her tried to point out. Except Darcy knew quite well that Will wanted to do everything she did, because she was his big sister and he wanted to be just as grown up as she was. And because Darcy was spending all her time on soccer, Will was, too. That's why he'd taken her ball and tried to play with it. Then while she was shouting at him about it, their kitten had given up on them and gone to find somewhere nicer to live. Somewhere where people actually wanted him around.

The tears spilled over and Darcy gasped out, "I don't think he wants us anymore!"

Mom and Dad had tried to convince Darcy that she was wrong and that Charlie loved their house, but it was harder and harder to do that when he still hadn't come home. And he didn't … all night.

"He doesn't even have his collar on," Darcy sobbed at bedtime. "We never remembered to go to the pet store and get him a new one. It's been days since he's had a collar. If he has found another home, the people probably think that he's a stray because they've never seen him with one."

"I wish he was better at keeping them on," Mom said, sighing.

Darcy gave a damp sort of laugh. "It isn't that he's bad at keeping them on, Mom. He takes them off on purpose. He's too clever. He rubs them against the chair legs until they come off." Her voice shook with tears again, and Mom hugged her tight. How could their smart, handsome, perfect kitten not want to be theirs anymore?

Later that night, she heard Mom and Dad talking when she went downstairs to get a drink of water. They were in the living room, and they didn't know she was there. Darcy sank down on the stairs and listened, peering through the banisters.

"Do you think Darcy's right?" Dad was asking. "Someone else has adopted him?"

She heard Mom sigh. "It's possible, isn't it? We have neglected him a bit—I just hadn't realized…. But to be honest, Dave, I'd rather he's being taken care of by someone than…. Well, cars go so quickly along this street, and he's so little. Cats are terrible with streets— they can't tell how fast the cars are."

"Someone would have come and told

us if he'd been hit, for sure. Oh—except he doesn't have his collar on."

"Exactly," Mom said grimly. "But hopefully anyone who picked him up would have taken him to the vet, and they'd scan his microchip. They'd call us."

"Mmmm. I suppose he could be shut in somewhere.... A shed, maybe, or a garage."

Darcy didn't want to listen anymore. She crept slowly back upstairs to bed, but after that it took a long time for her to get to sleep. She lay there, imagining Charlie trapped in a dark shed, mewing and mewing for her to come and let him out. Or frozen in the headlights of a car.... That was too horrible. She buried her head in her pillow, trying not to think about it.

She still woke up early the next morning, though. They all did. Last night they'd walked up and down the street, peering over fences and walls and calling for Charlie. They'd asked all the neighbors they'd seen, but no one had spotted a kitten. They just had to keep trying, Dad said firmly. He had to be somewhere.

"We should find a photo of Charlie and make a poster," Mom suggested.

"Oh! Can we do it now?" Darcy asked, jumping up. She'd been trying to eat a piece of toast because Mom had said she must eat something, but it just wasn't going down.

"You hardly ate anything last night...," Mom started to say, but then she shook

93

her head and sighed. "Actually, I'm not very hungry, either. All right. Let's look through my phone for a good photo."

Darcy and Will peered over Mom's shoulder, looking at photos of Charlie. There were so many—Charlie splayed out on the couch, legs everywhere; Charlie sitting in a cereal bowl Mom had left on the table; Charlie asleep with his nose in his food dish. Darcy felt her eyes prickling with tears again— she had to stop! It was no use crying; it wasn't going

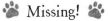

to help them find their kitten. She sniffed hard and pointed to a photo of Charlie staring out hopefully. He must have been waiting for his dinner or maybe a treat. It showed off his beautiful big yellow-green eyes and his tabby and white coloring.

"Yes, that's a good one," Mom agreed. "I'll download it onto my computer, and we'll make it into a poster." She went to turn on the computer, and Darcy followed her.

"What are we going to say?" she asked Mom. "I mean, if we think someone might have adopted Charlie, what we really want to say is 'Give us our cat back!' But I suppose we can't...."

"We don't know for sure that that's what happened," Mom pointed out.

"Though it does seem likely. What about this?" She typed quickly and then leaned back so Darcy could see.

LOST

Young tabby and white cat.
Charlie won't wear a collar
so he may look like a stray, but
he is a much-loved family pet.
Please help us find him!

"It's perfect," Darcy agreed.

Mom added her cell phone number and printed out twenty copies. "We'll start with these. If we don't hear anything, maybe we should do some smaller ones to put in all our neighbors' mailboxes."

Darcy nodded, swallowing hard. It had just hit her that they were really going to put up these posters—people were going to look at them and think, *Oh, I must keep an eye out for that poor little cat.* Of course, that was a good thing, but it was horrible that they had to do it. She had walked past so many posters just like this one and felt sorry for the poor lost cat and the sad owners, and now *they* were the sad owners.

"We're going to keep looking, too,

though, aren't we?" she said to Mom. "We only did our street yesterday. We should go to Third Street, too, and the one where the houses back up to our yards—Garland Court, isn't it?"

"We will, don't worry," Mom said. "We can look all morning, but then we've got to take you to your soccer game."

Darcy stared at her. She had completely forgotten about the soccer game! She shook her head. "I can't! Not when Charlie's missing, Mom. I just can't. Please will you tell Mrs. Jennings I can't go?"

Mom looked at her worriedly. "I'm not sure we should do that, sweetheart. You're part of a team. You'll be letting everyone else down."

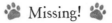

"I won't—it will just mean Emma gets more of a chance to play. Honestly, she'll be really happy. Don't you see? I stopped taking care of Charlie properly because I was so caught up with the soccer team. I was practicing all the time and not bothering to play with him. But now I don't care if I never get to be on the team again, if only we can find Charlie and he's safe."

Mom sighed. "Okay. Maybe I won't tell Mrs. Jennings exactly that, but hopefully she'll understand."

Chapter Seven
Looking for Charlie

Charlie had meant to go home—after a little while. Once he'd given Darcy and Will time to calm down and stop shouting. When they were arguing, it made the fur on the back of his neck rise up, and it hurt his ears. He'd never bitten Darcy or Will, and he'd never wanted to, except sometimes when they were yelling at each other and the anger seemed to be in the air all around them. Then it made him want to nip their ankles. It was better to just not be there.

When the elderly lady came home with a couple of shopping bags, she'd laughed to see him curled up and snoozing on her rug. She crouched down with great effort, rubbed his ears, and spoke softly to him, telling him how handsome and what nice company he was.

"There I was feeling lonely, and now you've come to see me," she told him.

Charlie sat up and purred, pushing his head affectionately into her hand and twining himself around her.

"It's a good thing I picked up a few more of those food packets, isn't it? Are you hungry, little one?" She stood up, and Charlie followed her eagerly into the kitchen. He *was* hungry. And after he'd eaten he was sleepy, and it was so nice to curl up on the lady's lap on the couch. He would go back later on, under the fence and over the wall, back to Darcy and Will.... But the apartment was cozy and quiet, and somehow, he just didn't.

Darcy listened to Mom's end of the phone conversation with Mrs. Jennings—she sounded very apologetic. She kept saying how much Darcy loved soccer, but it was just that this was important and everyone was very upset.

At that point, Darcy put one of the couch cushions over her head. It was too weird listening to Mom describe how miserable she was. It made her feel even sadder. The more people who knew that Charlie was missing, the worse it felt. *And now a bunch of people are going to know,* Darcy thought, sighing into the dusty fabric of the cushion.

Dad thought putting small versions of the poster in people's mailboxes was a very good idea. The neighbors would have a copy of the flyer with their phone number on it if they spotted Charlie, he pointed out, and Darcy knew they wanted as many people as possible to look for Charlie. But when everyone on the street was getting a little photo of Charlie in their mailbox, it made him seem a lot more missing.

She and Dad took turns doing the houses on their side of the street, while Mom and Will did the other side. Will was enjoying it, Darcy noticed sadly. He thought it was exciting, getting to put the little notes in the mailboxes. If it had been anything else they were handing out, Darcy would have liked it, too. But she seemed to keep catching the photo of Charlie at just the wrong angle—he looked so sad as she squashed him into the mailbox, his nose wrinkling up, his whiskers drooping. He looked like a Lost Cat.

They worked their way down the street to the side road, Third Street, which led to Garland Court—a mirror image of their street, with its yards joining on to theirs.

"We definitely need to deliver flyers along here," Darcy said to Dad. "Charlie was out in the yard, so he could easily have gone over the back fence into one of the yards here."

"Do you think so?" Dad said doubtfully. "Our back fence is pretty high. I'm not sure he could get over it, to be honest. I'd have thought he went up the side alley and out through the front yard."

Darcy shook her head. She'd seen Charlie scrambling up the side wall before and shooting up a tree as if it was a little cat ladder. He was an amazingly good climber.

"But maybe you're right," Dad said. "And it's not that far away—he could even have walked down the street and around the corner, like we did. Do we have enough flyers left, or do we need to go back and print some more?"

"Just about enough," Darcy said, showing him her handful. "Except there's the little block of apartments that almost backs up to us. I don't know how many people live there."

"Well, let's see how far we get," Dad said, heading up the path of the nearest house.

They still had a few flyers left when they got to the apartments at the end of the street, and Darcy looked at the main door uncertainly. It didn't have a mailbox—should they just leave the flyers on the front porch? But wouldn't they blow away?

"Do you think we should put them under the doors of the apartments?" she asked Dad. "There's no mail on Sundays, is there? No one is going to check those." She pointed to the group of mailboxes just down the street.

"We want them to look in the yard for Charlie today…. I wonder which apartment has the yard. Or maybe they share it?"

"Probably that one." Dad held the main door open and walked over to the door behind the staircase. "Put a flyer under here, Darcy."

But as Darcy crouched down to slide the flyer under the door, the lock clicked, and the door started to open.

A friendly voice said, "Hello! I heard you talking—are you delivering something?" But Darcy wasn't listening because right there, almost nose to nose, was a small tabby and white cat, staring curiously at her with round, yellow-green eyes.

Darcy was so surprised that she half fell over backward. "Charlie!" she cried loudly, and the tabby and white cat turned tail and raced back into the apartment.

"Was that Charlie?" Dad exclaimed. "Are you okay, love? Did you hurt yourself? I didn't see—was that him?"

Darcy only nodded. She couldn't speak. She was sure it had been Charlie, but he had taken one look at her and run away!

"Charlie?" The lady at the door looked anxiously between Darcy and her dad. "I'm sorry, I don't quite…. Oh!" She stared in surprise as Darcy scrambled up and raced away, pushing past Dad and out the main door, running for home.

Charlie was in the kitchen of the apartment, hunched up in a little ball under the table. His ears were flattened back, and his tail was double its usual size. He was confused. He hadn't expected to see Darcy here—she belonged in his other house. He had been missing her. He'd wanted to go back, but the windows had been closed overnight and there wasn't a cat flap here, like there was at home.

He hadn't minded all that much, since the elderly lady had made such a fuss of him and kept giving him little treats. She'd even bought a ball that rattled when he batted it and a litter box to go in the corner of her kitchen. But he'd kept thinking about Darcy and Will, and how good it would be to snuggle up on the end of Darcy's bed. He'd sat on the windowsill looking out at the dark yard and mewed a little, but the lady had petted him and tickled under his chin, and he'd forgotten....

Then to see Darcy when the door opened, that hadn't been right. He didn't understand—and she had shouted! He didn't even understand why he'd run....

But Darcy was gone again, and now he wished he hadn't dashed away from her....

The lady hurried into the kitchen, calling, "Kitty! Come on, little one. Oh, dear...."

Charlie eyed her, confused. She didn't sound right, either—she wasn't shouting, but her soft voice was high and anxious now.

The lady sat down on one of the kitchen chairs and sighed. Then she leaned over and peered at him under the table, looking between him and the piece of paper in her hand. "This is you, isn't it,

112

kitty? The little girl dropped it when she fell over. Oh, this is awful. I was so sure you were a stray when you kept coming back, and you seemed so hungry…. I suppose I just wanted you not to have a home so you could stay with me."

Charlie crept closer, nudging the piece of paper with his nose.

"Yes, that's definitely a picture of you. Well, we'd better take you back. That poor girl; she was so upset. They're from the house over the fence. I've heard them in the yard, the girl and her little brother."

Charlie put his front paws up against the lady's knee and tried to nibble the paper, but she scooped him up, cuddling him against her shoulder and rubbing the soft velvet of his nose. "I really must take you back. Oh, dear…."

Chapter Eight
Home Again

Darcy raced down the street toward home. She wasn't thinking very clearly—she was too upset to think. She just wanted to get away. That lady had stolen Charlie! She had kept him in her apartment and made him her cat instead. "She stole him! She stole him!" Darcy whispered shakily to herself as she ran.

But the problem was, even though she was upset, Darcy knew that wasn't really what had happened. It was only what she wanted to believe. If that lady *had* taken Charlie and kept him there when he hadn't wanted it, he would have raced away as soon as she opened the door. He hadn't been trying to escape when Darcy saw him—he'd just wanted to see who was at the door. It had been Darcy who'd upset him. He'd actually run away from *her*.

The lady had adopted him. She'd probably thought he didn't have a home because he'd kept showing up in her yard, and he didn't have a collar on. They had neglected him, all of them, but especially Darcy, and Charlie had gone looking for someone to love him.

Darcy sniffed hard. He'd found someone, and he'd chosen them instead.

She shoved the front gate open and stumbled up the path. Then she realized that of course the front door was locked, and Dad had the keys.

Darcy sank down on the doorstep, the last copy of their flyer in her hands. She stared at it and a fat tear splashed onto the photo of Charlie, blotching his beautiful pink nose. How could they have been so selfish and forgotten how special he was?

"Darcy!" Dad came hurrying down the path with Mom and Will close behind him.

"What happened?" Mom demanded. "We saw you running along the street! What's wrong? Did you find him? Oh, he's not...." She stopped herself, but Darcy knew what she had been going to say—she was worried that Charlie might have been hit by a car.

Darcy sniffed. If that had happened, it would be so much worse. She felt a tiny bit more cheerful—at least Charlie was safe.

Dad reached over her to unlock the front door. "Come on, we'll explain." He pulled Darcy up gently and led her inside.

"Did you find him?" Will asked.

"What happened? Why's Darcy crying? Where's Charlie?"

"At the apartment complex," Darcy sniffed. "With an elderly lady. He doesn't want to be our cat anymore." She pressed her hands against her eyes. "But at least he hasn't been run over, like Mom thought."

"What?" Mom put an arm around her. "Oh, Darcy, were you listening to me and Dad last night?"

"I didn't mean to," Darcy muttered shakily. Then she jumped as the doorbell rang shrilly, just behind them.

Will opened the door and stood staring at the lady on the doorstep—Charlie was clutched tightly in her arms.

She held him out, looking anxious, and Charlie wriggled.

"I'm so sorry. I'm Rose Macaulay, and I think this must be your cat."

Charlie nibbled at the little pile of cat food he'd left in his food bowl the day before, but the elderly lady had fed him that morning, and he wasn't very hungry. He padded around the kitchen, inspecting everyone's feet approvingly. They were all home, just where they should be. He nuzzled against Will's sneakers, and Will leaned down to pet him. Charlie let Will pet him for a minute and then sprang up onto Darcy's lap, expecting to be petted. Darcy always fussed over him.

But she only stared at him. Her hand lifted uncertainly as though she wanted to pet him but wasn't sure if she should. Charlie gazed back at her, remembering the way she'd yelled at Will the day before and then shouted at him when he peered around the door. Maybe she didn't want him after all! He laid his ears flat and crouched a little, wondering if he should jump down.

Slowly, hesitantly, Darcy reached to

rub his ears, and Charlie nudged his chin against her hand. No, it was all right. She was just the same as before. He closed his eyes and lifted his chin blissfully to the ceiling as she scratched him underneath. That was the exact place—no, there.... He began to purr.

"I'm so, so sorry," Rose was explaining. "He didn't have a collar on, and he looked so hungry." She sighed. "Of course, I'm sure he wasn't hungry at all. I guess he's just a very good actor. I never should have let him in that first day...."

"It's our fault," Mom said guiltily, turning around from filling the kettle for tea. "Everyone's been so busy since Darcy and Will went back to school. I should have realized that Charlie was wandering off. But I was occupied with work, and we just didn't pay him enough attention."

"Well, of course I won't feed him anymore. And if he comes into my yard again, I'll shoo him away," Rose said, looking down at Charlie, who was curled up on Darcy's lap now, a little tabby and white bundle. Darcy saw her face twist sadly.

"You don't need to do that!" she said in a whisper, so as not to disturb the dozing kitten, and Rose looked at her in surprise. "I mean—Charlie likes you. He's allowed to have friends...." Darcy shrugged, looking embarrassed. She knew what she meant, but it sounded a bit silly.

"Darcy's right," Dad said, smiling. "If you don't mind him inviting himself in, that is."

Rose smiled rather shyly. "That's very kind of you. I still feel awful about accidentally stealing your cat...."

"You should," Will said, glaring at her accusingly. "We were really worried about him!"

"Will!" Darcy gave him a shocked look. "Don't be so rude!"

But Rose shook her head, smiling. "Will reminds me very much of my grandson, Louis. He's seven."

Will looked happy. "I'm only six, but I'm really big. Does Louis go to the same school as us? There's a Louis in second grade, isn't there, Darcy?"

"No." Rose shook her head sadly. "He lives in London, I'm afraid, quite a long way away. But I get to talk to him on the phone every week."

Darcy looked down at Charlie and rubbed the fine puffs of fur just at the bottom of his ears. She couldn't help wondering if Rose was lonely, since her family didn't live close by. It felt as if she needed Charlie almost as much as they did.

"Charlie's very bad about keeping his collar on," she explained to Rose. "Do you think we could give you a spare collar, in case he comes over to you and he doesn't have one on?"

"Oh, of course!" Rose nodded delightedly. "I'll make sure to check." She leaned over to look at Charlie on Darcy's lap. "He really is a handsome one, isn't he?" she said admiringly.

Darcy nodded. "The most handsome cat ever." She wasn't sure if Charlie heard her, but he made a little *prrp* noise in his sleep and turned over on her lap, so he was lying on his back with his perfectly pink paws in the air. His tummy was all white fluff, with just a few patches of tabby spots around the edge.

"Oh, the angel," Rose said, laughing, and Darcy smiled down at Charlie, heavy and saggy and warm in her lap. Charlie was their cat—but she didn't mind sharing him, just a little.

HOLLY WEBB

Holly Webb started out as a children's book editor, and wrote her first series for the publisher she worked for. She has been writing ever since, with more than 100 books to her name. Holly lives in England with her husband, three children, and several cats who are always nosing around when she is trying to type on her laptop.

For more information
about Holly Webb visit:

www.holly-webb.com
www.tigertalesbooks.com